As the snow fell on the Yucky Mart, Putrid Pizza told the Grossery Gang, "Christmas will soon be here!"

"What's Christmas?" asked Rotten Egg, the youngest of the gang.

"Only the very best time!" shouted Dodgey Donut. "I know, let's have the grossest party ever!"

Being the Big Cheese, Putrid Pizza declared himself head of Pukey Party Planning.

"We'll need food, decorations, and music," he told them all.

"Apple pies with flies, and Christmas pudding with lots of moldy cheese sauce for me!" cried Fungus Fries.

Shoccoli, the stinky broccoli, took charge of the decorations, and in no time there were fantastic Christmas lights up all oozing slime.

Next, he set up the music.

"I suppose we have to listen to boring Christmas carols?" asked Sticky Soda, pretending she didn't want to have a party.

"Of course not," Dodgey Donut replied, dancing in
an extremely dodgy way.
Flies buzzed all around him.
"We're having rowdy rotten rhythms!"
He laughed as the music blasted.

"Time for the first party game!" shouted Putrid Pizza.
"It's red light, green light," he told them.

Everyone immediately started to jiggle about. Even Blue Spew Cheese jumped around as if he were a young, fresh dairy product again. Sticky Soda burped so much from all her stale fizz, that she kept leaping into the air.

Rotten Egg giggled helplessly at the sight of all his friends. He rolled right across the floor, leaving a trail of foul, sticky green yolk.

The Grossery Gang was having the time of their lives!

But then Squished Banana suddenly stopped the music and no one was able to keep still. It was hard when there were flies buzzing all around them.

For Sticky Soda, it was impossible because she couldn't stop burping up a foul taste.

Fungus Fries did manage to keep still for a moment or two, but then Rotten Egg rolled right into him. How could he keep still with all those vile green vapors coming up right under his nose?

"I don't think red light, green light is the right game for us," said Shoccoli, who was as wise as he was smelly.

"Yes, you're probably right," Putrid Pizza admitted, desperately trying to think of another party game for them.

"I know!" he said. "Musical chairs!"

"What's musical chairs?" asked Flat Battery.

Putrid Pizza found explaining the game almost as tough as his cheese topping.

Soon the gang was all running around the chairs, colliding into each other as the music played.

Gunk and sticky goo flew everywhere. The faster the music played, the more manic Fungus Fries became. But when Rotten Egg rolled underneath him again, he was not happy.

"Look what you've done!" Fungus Fries moaned.
"There's yolk all over me."

"Er—reality check!" Grub Sub chuckled. He pointed to the fries that were moldy and brown, and had maggots crawling over them.

"You were never the tastiest dish anyway!"

The gang ran around the chairs, growing more and more exhausted. The floor was getting stickier and stickier. Dodgey Donut was so busy dancing to the rotten rhythm, that he forgot to pause the music. Finally, he remembered.

Everyone tried to plop themselves down onto a chair.

Poor Blue Spew Cheese was left standing, sweating from every stinky pore and drooping even more than usual.

"I'm getting too old for party games," he wheezed.

"We all are," Putrid Pizza chuckled. "That's why we're way past our sell-by dates!"

"Let's play musical chairs again!" cried Flat Battery, starting the music once more. Everyone stayed on their chairs.

"Come on, gang," called Flat Battery. "Don't be lazy."

But no one could move.

Putrid Pizza was getting stuck from his sweating moldy cheese, Sticky Soda from her syrup puddles, and Fungus Fries from his dribbling green ketchup, which had set like glue.

So that was another party game that didn't work for the Grossery Gang!

"I know what will work," said Grub Sub. "Let's play blind man's bluff." He explained to Rotten Egg that all the gang had to do was take turns closing their eyes, touching someone, and then guessing who it was.

Rotten Egg thought this sounded like the best game of all.

Sticky Soda thought the same, but didn't want to show her excitement.

"I bet this game doesn't work either," she said.

Sticky Soda was right.

Once Squished Banana closed his eyes and touched someone, he immediately shouted, "It's Putrid Pizza!"

"You rotten cheater," protested Putrid Pizza. "You must have peeked."

"I might be rotten," Squished Banana said, "but I'm not a cheater. I would know that pukey cheese and mushroom smell anywhere."

When it was Putrid Pizza's turn to close his eyes, he too could tell who he was touching.

"Sewer Glove!" he cried out correctly.

It turned out that this party game didn't work for the Grossery Gang either. But then Shoccoli thought of a brand-new game.

"It's called blind man's stink," he explained. "You play it the same way, but this time, the blind man also puts a clothespin on his nose."

But the clothespin did not make the game any harder. Everyone was so smelly from all the running around at the party, they could easily figure out everyone's smell.

Even though they couldn't come up with a game everyone liked, they all agreed it was still the grossest party ever!

"I love Christmas parties!" cried Rotten Egg, before rolling into the corner and falling fast asleep.

MERRY GROSS CHRISTMAS, EVERYONE!